For my wonderful agent, Becky Bagnell. — D.D.

For Emma Rose Glover

love Great Uncle Freddie xx— F.B.

First published 2022 by Macmillan Children's Books
an imprint of Pan Macmillan
The Smithson, 6 Briset Street, London, EC1M 5NR
EU representative: Macmillan Publishers Ireland Ltd, 1st Floor,
The Liffey Trust Centre, 117-126 Sheriff Street Upper,
Dublin 1, D01 YC43
Associated companies throughout the world
www.panmacmillan.com

ISBN: 978-1-5290-4949-7

Text copyright © Donna David 2022
Illustrations copyright © Fred Blunt 2022
Moral rights asserted.

3 5 7 9 8 6 4 2

A CIP catalogue record for this book is available from the British Library.

Printed in China

FSC
www.fsc.org

MIX
Paper from
responsible sources
FSC® C116313

Farmer Llama

Donna David · Fred Blunt

MACMILLAN CHILDREN'S BOOKS

Alarm-a-Llama bolts awake
And bashes his poor head.

Pyjama-Llama rubs his eyes
And climbs out of his bed.

Banana-Llama grabs some food.

He's ready for the day!

Farmer-Llama starts his truck
And heads out to collect hay.

Drama-Llama screams in shock—
The cows are on the run!

Screeechhh

Harm-a-Llama yelps in pain—
That one just charged his bum!

Arm-a-Llama grabs a stick.
He's ready to attack!

Disarm-a-Llama flies so high,
And lands flat on his back!

Charmer-Llama has a plan.
He wafts round yummy snacks.

Bahama-Llama doesn't mind.
He'll kick back and relax.

Calmer-Llama sighs, "At last!
Those cows made me so stressed!"

Mama-Llama calls out, "Thanks . . .
. . . Now please go fetch the rest!"

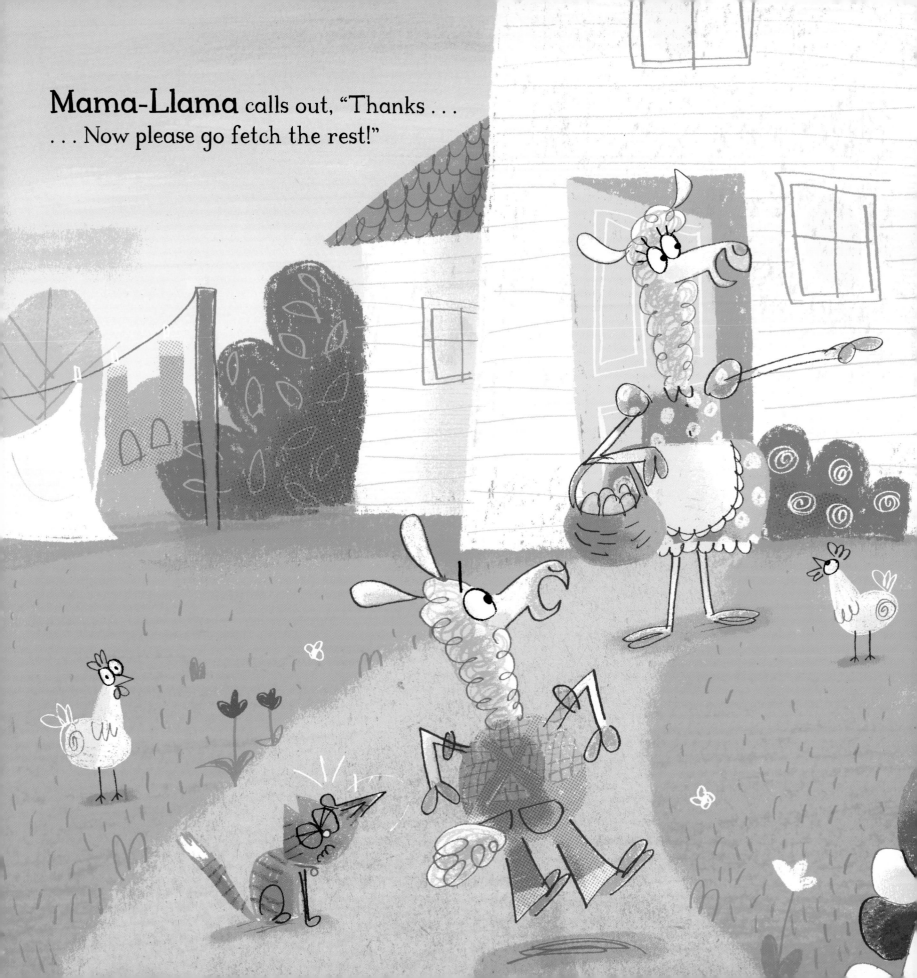